DISNEP

BEAUTY AND THE BEAST

SOMETHING MORE

By ERIC GERON

Screenplay by EVAN SPILIOTOPOULOS
and STEPHEN CHBOSKY and BILL CONDON

SUSTAINABLE
FORESTRY
INITIATIVE

Certified Sourcing

www.sfiprogram.org
SFI-01415

DISNEP PRESS

LOS ANGELES • NEW YORK

Printed in the United States of America

First Paperback Edition, January 2017

3 5 7 9 10 8 6 4

Library of Congress Control Number: 2016952970

FAC-029261-17059

ISBN 978-1-4847-8284-2

For more Disney Press fun, visit www.disneybooks.com

For more *Beauty and the Beast* fun, visit www.disney.com/beautyandthebeast

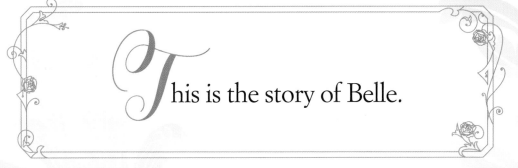

This is the story of Belle.

Belle was smart.

She loved to read.

Belle carried books everywhere.

She read about far-off places.

Like always, Belle bought bread from the baker.

Every day was the same in the small village.
She longed for something more. . . .

The villagers did not understand Belle. They said she was different.

Belle held her head high. She was brave.

Belle was also kind.

She gave her bread and jam to a beggar.

Villagers saw Belle reading. They called her odd.

Belle tried to ignore the villagers.
But she wondered if they were right.

A man named Gaston also saw Belle.

Gaston was a rude brute. His best friend was LeFou.

Gaston thought Belle
was beautiful.

He wanted to marry
Belle for her looks.

Gaston asked Belle to dinner, and Belle said no. He did not see Belle for her beauty within.

Belle hoped one day someone would understand her. She longed for something more. . . .

Belle talked with her father, Maurice. He told Belle that she was fearless and daring.

Maurice told Belle to ignore the villagers. He loved that his daughter was different.

Belle loved her father very much. He made her feel like she belonged.

He and his horse, Philippe, were leaving for the market. Belle said good-bye to them.

The next day, Philippe returned to the village.

Maurice was nowhere to be found.

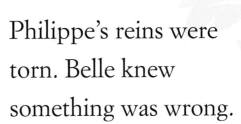

Philippe's reins were torn. Belle knew something was wrong.

She set out to find her father.

Clues led Belle into a strange castle.
She knew her father must be inside.

But she did not know what else she would find. . . .

Belle was smart and brave and kind.
She soon found out the castle was
enchanted. Her fairy tale was about to
begin.